VIKING

Published by the Penguin Group
Penguin Books USA Inc., 375 Hudson Street, New York, New York 10014, U.S.A.
Penguin Books Ltd, 27 Wrights Lane, London W8 5TZ, England
Penguin Books Australia Ltd, Ringwood, Victoria, Australia
Penguin Books Canada Ltd, 10 Alcorn Avenue, Toronto, Ontario, Canada M4V 3B2
Penguin Books (N.Z.) Ltd, 182-190 Wairau Road, Auckland 10, New Zealand

Penguin Books Ltd, Registered Offices: Harmondsworth, Middlesex, England

First published in 1996 in Great Britain by Hodder Children's Books, a division of Hodder Headline plc
First published in 1997 in the United States of America by Viking, a division of Penguin Books USA Inc.
Published by arrangement with Hodder Children's Books

3 5 7 9 10 8 6 4 2

LIBRARY OF CONGRESS CATALOG CARD NUMBER: 96-60042   ISBN 0-670-87034-X

Manufactured in China   Set in Bembo

Bearobics

A Hip-Hop Counting Story

Vic Parker
Emily Bolam

VIKING

Deep in the forest there's a
thumping, bumping sound,
A drumming and a humming, a stomping on the ground.
The pumping rumpus rhythm takes control of both your feet
And suddenly you find yourself getting with the beat.
But where's that boogie coming from,
That rapping in the air?

From out of the boom box of **One** shaggy bear.

Come on everybody! Do that **wild Bear**obics thing.

Let yourself go! Get into the **swing!**

With a **fizzle** in their fingers and a **tingle** in their toes,

TWO hoppin' kangaroos know how Bearobics goes.

Three giggling gorillas now get into the groove.

Bopping and shoowapping.
Just watch them as they move!

Going to a **go-go**, **four** ostriches arrive

To show off *fancy* footwork in the jumping jungle jive.

With a stripy shoulder Shimmy, yelling out for more,

Five funky tigers fandango on the floor.

Six lazzzzzzzy snakes, hissssssing with delight,

Do a hippy hippy shake to the left and to the right.

Seven swinging penguins can't get quite enough.

With a slide to the side they shake and strut their stuff.

Going even *faster* now—mustn't stop to rest—

Jumping in a jumble,
Eight bunnies bounce the best.

The pace is really pounding—get ready for **high** kicks.

Nine *flashy* frogs go crazy with their lively leggy tricks.

Ten dizzy mice disco in and seize the chance

To jitterbug and tango in the great Bearobics dance.

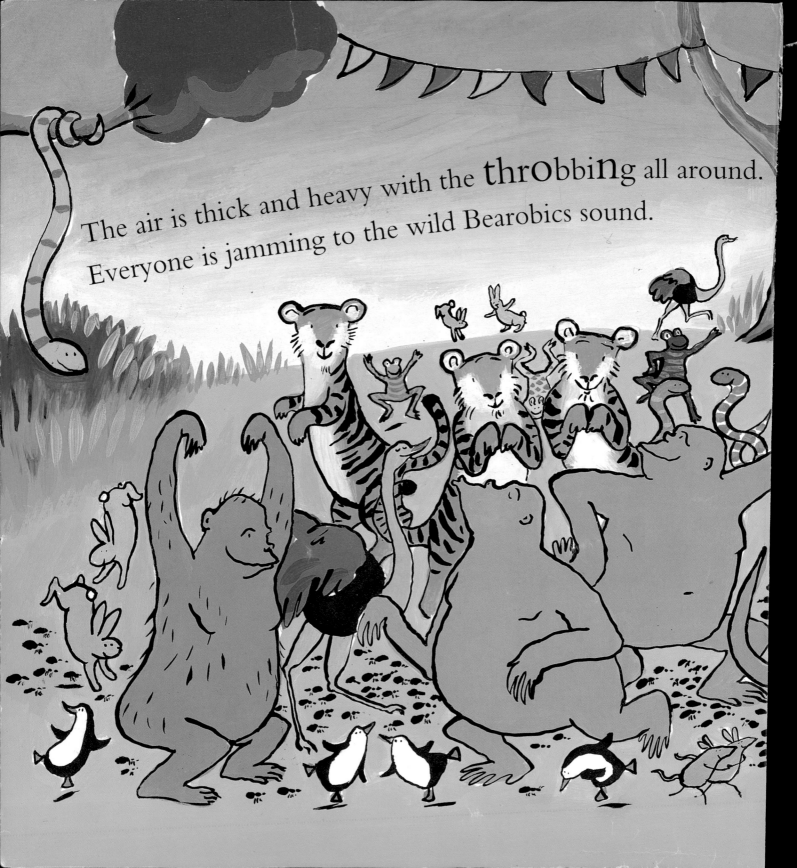

The air is thick and heavy with the **throbbing** all around.
Everyone is jamming to the wild Bearobics sound.

Once you try Bearobics, you'll never want to stop.
Just rap to this Bearobics beat and dance
until you drop!